'People begin to see that something more goes to the composition of a fine murder than two blockheads to kill and be killed – a knife – a purse – and a dark lane . . .'

THOMAS DE QUINCEY
Born 1785, Manchester, England
Died 1859, Edinburgh, Scotland

In December 1811, a series of brutal murders was carried out
in Ratcliffe Highway, in London's East End. The presumed
murderer, John Williams, was arrested on 22 December and
found hanged in his cell a few days later. De Quincey was
haunted by the crime, and returned to it many times in his
writing over the next thirty years. This essay first appeared
in *Blackwood's Magazine* in February 1827.

DE QUINCEY IN PENGUIN CLASSICS
Confessions of an English Opium-Eater and Other Writings

THOMAS DE QUINCEY

On Murder Considered as One of the Fine Arts

PENGUIN BOOKS

PENGUIN CLASSICS

UK | USA | Canada | Ireland | Australia
India | New Zealand | South Africa

Penguin Books is part of the Penguin Random House group of companies
whose addresses can be found at global.penguinrandomhouse.com.

This selection published in Penguin Classics 2015
003

Set in 10/14.5 pt Baskerville 10 Pro
Typeset by Jouve (UK), Milton Keynes
Printed in Great Britain by Clays Ltd, St Ives plc

A CIP catalogue record for this book is available from the British Library

ISBN: 978-0-141-39788-7

www.greenpenguin.co.uk

Penguin Random House is committed to a
sustainable future for our business, our readers
and our planet. This book is made from Forest
Stewardship Council® certified paper.

TO THE EDITOR OF BLACKWOOD'S MAGAZINE

Sir,

We have all heard of a Society for the Promotion of Vice, of the Hell-Fire Club, &c. At Brighton I think it was that a Society was formed for the Suppression of Virtue. That Society was itself suppressed – but I am sorry to say that another exists in London, of a character still more atrocious. In tendency, it may be denominated a Society for the Encouragement of Murder; but, according to their own delicate ευφημισμὸς [euphemism], it is styled – The Society of Connoisseurs in Murder. They profess to be curious in homicide; amateurs and dilettanti in the various modes of bloodshed; and, in short, Murder-Fanciers. Every fresh atrocity of that class, which the police annals of Europe bring up, they meet and criticise as they would a picture, statue, or other work of art. But I need not trouble myself with any attempt to describe the spirit of their proceedings, as you will collect *that* much better from one of the Monthly Lectures read before the Society last year. This has fallen into my hands accidentally, in spite of all the vigilance exercised to keep their transactions from the public eye. The publication of it will alarm them; and my purpose is that it should. For I would much rather put them down quietly, by an appeal to public opinion through you, than by such an exposure of names as would follow an appeal to Bow-street; which last appeal, however, if this should fail, I must positively resort to. For it is scandalous that such things should go on in a Christian land. Even in a heathen land, the public toleration of murder was felt by a Christian writer to be the most crying reproach of the public morals. This writer was Lactantius; and with his words, as singularly applicable to the present occasion, I shall conclude: – 'Quid tam horribile,' says he, 'tam tetrum, quam hominis trucidatio? Ideo severissimis legibus vita nostra munitur; ideo bella execrabilia sunt. Invenit tamen consuetudo quatenus homicidium sine bello ac sine legibus faciat: et hoc sibi voluptas quod scelus

vindicavit. Quod si interesse homicidio sceleris con-
scientia est, – et eidem facinori spectator obstrictus
est cui et admissor; ergo et in his gladiatorum caedibus
non minus cruore profunditur qui spectat, quam ille
qui facit: nec potest esse immunis à sanguine qui voluit
effundi; aut videri non interfecisse, qui interfectori et
favit et proemium postulavit.' 'Human life,' says he,
'is guarded by laws of the uttermost rigour, yet custom
has devised a mode of evading them in behalf of murder; and the demands of taste (*voluptas*) are now
become the same as those of abandoned guilt.' Let the
Society of Gentlemen Amateurs consider this; and let
me call their especial attention to the last sentence,
which is so weighty, that I shall attempt to convey it
in English: – 'Now, if merely to be present at a murder
fastens on a man the character of an accomplice, – if
barely to be a spectator involves us in one common
guilt with the perpetrator; it follows of necessity, that,
in these murders of the amphitheatre, the hand which
inflicts the fatal blow is not more deeply imbrued in
blood than his who sits and looks on; neither can *he*
be clear of blood who has countenanced its shedding;
nor that man seem other than a participator in murder
who gives his applause to the murderer, and calls for

3

prizes in his behalf.' The '*proemia postulavit*' ['call for prizes'] I have not yet heard charged upon the Gentlemen Amateurs of London, though undoubtedly their proceedings tend to that; but the '*interfectori favit*' ['applause to the murderer'] is implied in the very title of this association, and expressed in every line of the lecture which I send you. – I am, &c.

X.Y.Z.

(*Note of the Editor*. – We thank our correspondent for his communication, and also for the quotation from Lactantius, which is very pertinent to *his* view of the case; our own, we confess, is different. We cannot suppose the lecturer to be in earnest, any more than Erasmus in his Praise of Folly, or Dean Swift in his proposal for eating children. However, either on his view or on ours, it is equally fit that the lecture should be made public.)

LECTURE

Gentlemen, – I have had the honour to be appointed by your committee to the trying task of reading the

Williams' Lecture on Murder, considered as one of the Fine Arts – a task which might be easy enough three or four centuries ago, when the art was little understood, and few great models had been exhibited; but in this age, when masterpieces of excellence have been executed by professional men, it must be evident, that in the style of criticism applied to them, the public will look for something of a corresponding improvement. Practice and theory must advance *pari passu* ['with an equal step']. People begin to see that something more goes to the composition of a fine murder than two blockheads to kill and be killed – a knife – a purse – and a dark lane. Design, gentlemen, grouping, light and shade, poetry, sentiment, are now deemed indispensable to attempts of this nature. Mr Williams has exalted the ideal of murder to all of us; and to me, therefore, in particular, has deepened the arduousness of my task. Like Aeschylus or Milton in poetry, like Michael Angelo in painting, he has carried his art to a point of colossal sublimity; and, as Mr Wordsworth observes, has in a manner 'created the taste by which he is to be enjoyed.' To sketch the history of the art, and to examine its principles critically, now remains as a duty for the connoisseur, and for judges of quite another stamp from his Majesty's Judges of Assize.

Before I begin, let me say a word or two to certain prigs, who affect to speak of our society as if it were in some degree immoral in its tendency. Immoral! – God bless my soul, gentlemen, what is it that people mean? I am for morality, and always shall be, and for virtue and all that; and I do affirm, and always shall, (let what will come of it,) that murder is an improper line of conduct – highly improper; and I do not stick to assert, that any man who deals in murder, must have very incorrect ways of thinking, and truly inaccurate principles; and so far from aiding and abetting him by pointing out his victim's hiding-place, as a great moralist* of Germany declared it to be every good man's duty to do, I would subscribe one shilling

---

* Kant – who carried his demands of unconditional veracity to so extravagant a length as to affirm, that, if a man were to see an innocent person escape from a murderer, it would be his duty, on being questioned by the murderer, to tell the truth, and to point out the retreat of the innocent person, under any certainty of causing murder. Lest this doctrine should be supposed to have escaped him in any heat of dispute, on being taxed with it by a celebrated French writer, he solemnly reaffirmed it, with his reasons.

and sixpence to have him apprehended, which is more by eighteen-pence than the most eminent moralists have subscribed for that purpose. But what then? Everything in this world has two handles. Murder, for instance, may be laid hold of by its moral handle, (as it generally is in the pulpit, and at the Old Bailey;) and *that*, I confess, is its weak side; or it may also be treated *aesthetically*, as the Germans call it, that is, in relation to good taste.

To illustrate this, I will urge the authority of three eminent persons, viz. S. T. Coleridge, Aristotle, and Mr Howship the surgeon. To begin with S.T.C. – One night, many years ago, I was drinking tea with him in Berners' Street, (which, by the way, for a short street, has been uncommonly fruitful in men of genius.) Others were there besides myself; and amidst some carnal considerations of tea and toast, we were all imbibing a dissertation on Plotinus from the attic lips of S.T.C. Suddenly a cry arose of '*Fire – fire!*' – upon which all of us, master and disciples, Plato and οἱ περί τον Πλάτωνα ['those around Plato'], rushed out, eager, for the spectacle. The fire was in Oxford Street, at a piano-forte maker's; and, as it promised to be a conflagration of merit, I was sorry that my engagements forced me away from Mr Coleridge's party before matters were come to a crisis. Some days after, meeting with my Platonic host, I reminded him of the case, and begged to know how that very promising exhibition had terminated. 'Oh, sir,' said he, 'it turned out so ill, that we damned it unanimously.' Now, does any man suppose that Mr Coleridge, – who, for all he is too fat to be a person of active virtue, is undoubtedly a worthy Christian, – that this good S.T.C., I say, was an incendiary, or capable of wishing any ill to the poor man and his piano-fortes (many of them, doubtless, with the additional keys)? On the contrary, I know him to be that sort of man that I durst stake my life upon it he would have worked an engine in a case of necessity, although rather of the fattest for such fiery trials of his virtue. But how stood the case? Virtue was in no request. On the arrival of the fire-engines, morality had devolved wholly on the insurance office. This being the case, he had a right to gratify his taste. He had left his tea. Was he to have nothing in return?

I contend that the most virtuous man, under the premises stated, was entitled to make a luxury of the fire, and to hiss it, as he would any other performance that raised expectations in the public mind, which afterwards it disappointed. Again, to cite another great authority, what says the Stagyrite? He (in the Fifth Book, I think it is, of his Metaphysics,) describes what he calls κλεπτὴν τέλειον, i.e. *a perfect thief*; and, as to Mr Howship, in a work of his on Indigestion, he makes no scruple to talk with admiration of a certain ulcer which he had seen, and which he styles 'a beautiful ulcer.' Now will any man pretend, that, abstractedly considered, a thief could appear to Aristotle a perfect character, or that Mr Howship could be enamoured of an ulcer? Aristotle, it is well known, was himself so very moral a character, that, not content with writing his Nichomachean Ethics, in one volume octavo, he also wrote another system, called *Magna Moralia*, or Big Ethics. Now, it is impossible that a man who composes any ethics at all, big or little, should admire a thief *per se*, and, as to Mr Howship, it is well known that he makes war upon all ulcers; and, without suffering himself to be seduced by their charms, endeavours to banish them from the county of Middlesex. But the truth is, that, however objectionable *per se*, yet, relatively to others of their class, both a thief and an ulcer may have infinite degrees of merit. They are both imperfections, it is true; but to be imperfect being their essence, the very greatness of their imperfection becomes their perfection. *Spartam nactus es, hanc exorna* ['Sparta is yours: adorn it!']. A thief like Autolycus or Mr Barrington, and a grim phagedaenic ulcer, superbly defined, and running regularly through all its natural stages, may no less justly be regarded as ideals after *their* kind, than the most faultless moss-rose amongst flowers, in its progress from bud to 'bright consummate flower;' or, amongst human flowers, the most magnificent young female, apparelled in the pomp of woman-hood. And thus not only the ideal of an inkstand may be imagined, (as Mr Coleridge demonstrated in his celebrated correspondence with Mr Blackwood,) in which, by the way, there is not so much, because an inkstand is a laudable sort of thing, and a valuable member of society; but even imperfection itself may have its ideal or perfect state.

Really, gentlemen, I beg pardon for so much philosophy at one time, and now, let me apply it. When a murder is in the paulo-post-futurum tense, and a rumour of it comes to our ears, by all means let us treat it morally. But suppose it over and done, and that you can say of it, Τετέλεσαι ['it is completed'] or (in that adamantine molossus of Medea) εἴργασαι ['it is done']; Suppose the poor murdered man to be out of his pain, and the rascal that did it off like a shot, nobody knows whither; suppose, lastly, that we have done our best, by putting out our legs to trip up the fellow in his flight, but all to no purpose – 'abiit, evasit' ['he has left, escaped'], &c. – why, then, I say, what's the use of any more virtue? Enough has been given to morality; now comes the turn of Taste and the Fine Arts. A sad thing it was, no doubt, very sad; but *we* can't mend it. Therefore let us make the best of a bad matter; and, as it is impossible to hammer anything out of it for moral purposes, let us treat it aesthetically, and see if it will turn to account in that way. Such is the logic of a sensible man, and what follows? We dry up our tears, and have the satisfaction perhaps to discover, that a transaction, which, morally considered, was shocking, and without a leg to stand upon, when tried by principles of Taste, turns out to be a very meritorious performance. Thus all the world is pleased; the old proverb is justified, that it is an ill wind which blows nobody good; the amateur, from looking bilious and sulky, by too close an attention to virtue, begins to pick up his crumbs, and general hilarity prevails. Virtue has had her day; and henceforward, *Vertu* and Connoisseurship have leave to provide for themselves. Upon this principle, gentlemen, I propose to guide your studies, from Cain to Mr Thurtell. Through this great gallery of murder, therefore, together let us wander hand in hand, in delighted admiration, while I endeavour to point your attention to the objects of profitable criticism.

The first murder is familiar to you all. As the inventor of murder, and the father of the art, Cain must have been a man of first-rate genius. All the Cains were men of genius. Tubal Cain invented tubes, I think, or some such thing. But, whatever were the originality and genius of the artist, every art was then in its infancy; and the works must be criticised with a re-collection of that fact. Even Tubal's work would probably be little approved at this day in Sheffield; and therefore of Cain (Cain senior, I mean,) it is no disparagement to say, that his performance was but so so. Milton, however, is supposed to have thought differently. By his way of relating the case, it should seem to have been rather a pet murder with him, for he retouches it with an apparent anxiety for its picturesque effect: –

> Whereat he inly raged; and, as they talk'd,
> Smote him into the midriff with a stone
> That beat out life: he fell; and, deadly pale,
> Groan'd out his soul *with gushing blood effus'd*.
>
> *Par. Lost*, B. XI.

Upon this, Richardson the painter, who had an eye for effect, remarks as follows, in his Notes on Paradise Lost, p. 497: – 'It has been thought,' says he, 'that Cain beat (as the common saying is,) the breath out of his brother's body with a great stone; Milton gives in to this, with the addition, however, of a large wound.' In this place it was a judicious addition; for the rudeness of the weapon, unless raised and enriched by a warm, sanguinary colouring, has too much of the naked air of the savage school; as if the deed were perpetrated by a Polypheme without science, premeditation, or anything but a mutton bone. However, I am chiefly pleased with the improvement, as it implies that Milton was an amateur. As to Shakspeare, there never was a better; as his description of the murdered Duke of Gloucester, in Henry VI., of Duncan's, Banquo's, &c. sufficiently proves.

The foundation of the art having been once laid, it is pitiable to see how it slumbered without improvement for ages. In fact, I shall now be obliged to leap over all murders, sacred and profane, as utterly unworthy of notice, until long after the Christian era. Greece, even in the age of Pericles, produced no murder of the slightest merit; and Rome had too little originality of genius in any of the arts to succeed, where her model failed her. In fact, the Latin language sinks under the very idea of murder. 'The man was murdered;' – how will this sound in Latin? *Interfectús est, interemptus est* [he was killed, he was destroyed] – which simply expresses a homicide; and hence the Christian Latinity of the middle ages was obliged to introduce a new word, such as the feebleness of classic conceptions never ascended to. *Murdratus est*, says the sublimer dialect of Gothic ages. Meantime, the Jewish school of murder kept alive whatever was yet known in the art, and gradually transferred it to the Western World. Indeed the Jewish school was always respectable, even in the dark ages, as the case of Hugh

of Lincoln shows, which was honoured with the
approbation of Chaucer, on occasion of another performance from the same school, which he puts into
the mouth of the Lady Abbess.

Recurring, however, for one moment to classical
antiquity, I cannot but think that Catiline, Clodius,
and some of that coterie, would have made first-rate
artists; and it is on all accounts to be regretted, that
the priggism of Cicero robbed his country of the only
chance she had for distinction in this line. As the *subject* of a murder, no person could have answered better
than himself. Lord! how he would have howled with
panic, if he had heard Cethegus under his bed. It
would have been truly diverting to have listened to
him; and satisfied I am, gentlemen, that he would
have preferred the *utile* [expediency] of creeping into
a closet, or even into a *cloaca* [sewer], to the *honestum*
[honourable thing] of facing the bold artist.

To come now to the dark ages – (by which we, that
speak with precision, mean, *par excellence*, the tenth
century, and the times immediately before and
after) – these ages ought naturally to be favourable
to the art of murder, as they were to church-architecture,
to stained-glass, &c.; and, accordingly, about the

latter end of this period, there arose a great character
in our art, I mean the Old Man of the Mountains.
He was a shining light, indeed, and I need not tell
you, that the very word 'assassin' is deduced from
him. So keen an amateur was he, that on one occasion, when his own life was attempted by a favourite
assassin, he was so much pleased with the talent
shown, that notwithstanding the failure of the artist,
he created him a Duke upon the spot, with remainder
to the female line, and settled a pension on him for
three lives. Assassination is a branch of the art which
demands a separate notice; and I shall devote an
entire lecture to it. Meantime, I shall only observe
how odd it is, that this branch of the art has flourished
by fits. It never rains, but it pours. Our own age can
boast of some fine specimens; and, about two centuries ago, there was a most brilliant constellation of
murders in this class. I need hardly say, that I allude
especially to those five splendid works, – the assassinations of William I. of Orange, of Henry IV. of
France, of the Duke of Buckingham, (which you will
find excellently described in the letters published by
Mr Ellis, of the British Museum,) of Gustavus
Adolphus, and of Wallenstein. The King of Sweden's

assassination, by the by, is doubted by many writers, Harte amongst others; but they are wrong. He was murdered; and I consider his murder unique in its excellence; for he was murdered at noon-day, and on the field of battle, – a feature of original conception, which occurs in no other work of art that I remember. Indeed, all of these assassinations may be studied with profit by the advanced connoisseur. They are all of them *exemplaria*, of which one may say, –

Nocturnâ versatâ manu, versate diurne;
['Let these be your models by day and by night']

Especially *nocturnâ*.

In these assassinations of princes and statesmen, there is nothing to excite our wonder: important changes often depend on their deaths; and, from the eminence on which they stand, they are peculiarly exposed to the aim of every artist who happens to be possessed by the craving for scenical effect. But there is another class of assassinations, which has prevailed from an early period of the seventeenth century, that really *does* surprise me; I mean the assassination of philosophers. For, gentlemen, it is a fact, that every philosopher of eminence for the two last centuries has either been murdered, or, at the least, been very near it; insomuch, that if a man calls himself a philosopher, and never had his life attempted, rest assured there is nothing in him; and against Locke's philosophy in particular, I think it an unanswerable objection, (if we needed any) that, although he carried his throat about with him in this world for seventy-two years, no man ever condescended to cut it. As these cases of philosophers are not much known, and are generally good and well composed in their circumstances, I shall here read an excursus on that subject, chiefly by way of showing my own learning.

The first great philosopher of the seventeenth century (if we except Galileo,) was Des Cartes; and if ever one could say of a man that he was all *but* murdered – murdered within an inch, one must say it of him. The case was this, as reported by Baillet in his *Vie De M. Des Cartes*, tom. I. pp. 102–3. In the year 1621, when Des Cartes might be about twenty-six years old, he was touring about as usual, (for he was as restless as a hyaena,) and, coming to the Elbe, either at Gluckstadt or at Hamburg, he took shipping for East Friezland: what he could want in East Friezland no man has ever discovered; and perhaps he took this into consideration himself; for, on reaching Embden, he resolved to sail instantly for *West* Friezland; and being very impatient of delay, he hired a bark, with a few mariners to navigate it. No sooner had he got out to sea than he made a pleasing discovery, viz. that he had shut himself up in a den of murderers. His crew, says M. Baillet, he soon found out to be 'des scélérats,' – not *amateurs*, gentlemen, as we are, but professional men – the height of whose ambition at that moment was to cut his throat. But the story is too pleasing to be abridged – I shall give it, therefore, accurately, from the French of his biographer: 'M. Des Cartes had no company but that of his servant, with whom he was conversing in French. The sailors, who took him for a foreign merchant, rather than a cavalier, concluded that he must have money about him. Accordingly they came to a resolution by no means advantageous to his purse. There is this difference, however, between sea-robbers and the robbers in forests, that the latter may, without hazard, spare the lives of their victims; whereas the other cannot put a passenger on shore in such a case without running the risk of being apprehended. The crew of M. Des Cartes arranged their measures with a view to evade any danger of that sort. They observed that he was a stranger from a distance, without acquaintance in the country, and that nobody would take any trouble to inquire about him, in case he should never come to hand, (*quand il viendroit à manquer*.)' Think, gentlemen, of these Friezland dogs discussing a philosopher as if he were a puncheon of rum. 'His temper, they remarked, was very mild and patient; and, judging from the gentleness of his deportment, and the courtesy with which he treated themselves, that he could be nothing more than some green young man, they concluded that they should have all the easier task in disposing of his life. They made no scruple to discuss the whole matter in his presence, as not supposing that he understood any other language than that in which he conversed with his servant; and the amount of their deliberation was – to murder him, then to throw him into the sea, and to divide his spoils.'

Excuse my laughing, gentlemen, but the fact is, I always *do* laugh when I think of this case – two things about it seem so droll. One is, the horrid panic or 'funk,' (as the men of Eton call it,) in which Des Cartes must have found himself upon hearing this regular drama sketched for his own death – funeral – succession and administration to his effects. But another thing, which seems to me still more funny about this affair is, that if these Friezland hounds had been 'game,' we should have no Cartesian philosophy; and how we could have done without *that*, considering the worlds of books it has produced, I leave to any respectable trunk-maker to declare.

However, to go on; spite of his enormous funk, Des Cartes showed fight, and by that means awed these Anti-Cartesian rascals. 'Finding,' says M. Baillet, 'that the matter was no joke, M. Des Cartes leaped upon his feet in a trice, assumed a stern countenance that these cravens had never looked for, and addressing them in their own language, threatened to run them through on the spot if they dared to offer him any insult.' Certainly, gentlemen, this would have been an honour far above the merits of such inconsiderable rascals – to be spitted like larks upon a Cartesian sword; and therefore I am glad M. Des Cartes did not rob the gallows by executing his threat, especially as he could not possibly have brought his vessel to port, after he had murdered his crew; so that he must have continued to cruise for ever in the

Zuyder Zee, and would probably have been mistaken by sailors for the *Flying Dutchman*, homeward-bound. 'The spirit which M. Des Cartes manifested,' says his biographer, 'had the effect of magic on these wretches. The suddenness of their consternation struck their minds with a confusion which blinded them to their advantage, and they conveyed him to his destination as peaceably as he could desire.'

Possibly, gentlemen, you may fancy that, on the model of Caesar's address to his poor ferryman, – '*Caesarem vehis et fortunas ejus,*' ['You carry Caesar and his fortunes'] – M. Des Cartes needed only to have said, – 'Dogs, you cannot cut my throat, for you carry Des Cartes and his philosophy,' and might safely have defied them to do their worst. A German emperor had the same notion, when, being cautioned to keep out of the way of a cannonading, he replied, 'Tut! man. Did you ever hear of a cannon-ball that killed an emperor?' As to an emperor I cannot say, but a less thing has sufficed to smash a philosopher; and the next great philosopher of Europe undoubtedly *was* murdered. This was Spinosa.

I know very well the common opinion about him is, that he died in his bed. Perhaps he did, but he was murdered for all that; and this I shall prove by a book published at Brussels, in the year 1731, entitled, *La Via de Spinosa; par M. Jean Colerus*, with many additions, from a MS. life, by one of his friends. Spinosa died on the 21st February 1677, being then little more than forty-four years old. This of itself looks suspicious; and M. Jean admits, that a certain expression in the MS. life of him would warrant the conclusion, 'que sa mort n'a pas été tout-à-fait naturelle.' Living in a damp country, and a sailor's country, like Holland, he may be thought to have indulged a good deal in grog, especially in punch,* which was then newly discovered. Undoubtedly he might have done so; but the fact is that he did not. M. Jean calls him 'extrêmement sobre en son boire et en son manger.' And though some wild stories were afloat about his

---

*   'June 1, 1675. – Drinke part of 3 boules of punch, (a liquor very strainge to me,)' says the Rev. Mr Henry Teonge, in his Diary lately published. In a note on this passage, a reference is made to Fryer's Travels to the East Indies, 1672, who speaks of 'that enervating liquor called *Paunch*, (which is Indostan for five,) from five ingredients.' Made thus, it seems the medical men called it Diapente; if with four only, Diatessaron. No doubt, it was its Evangelical name that recommended it to the Rev. Mr Teonge.

using the juice of mandragora (p. 140,) and opium, (p. 144,) yet neither of these articles appeared in his druggist's bill. Living, therefore, with such sobriety, how was it possible that he should die a natural death at forty-four? Hear his biographer's account: – 'Sunday morning the 21st of February, before it was church-time, Spinosa came down stairs and conversed with the master and mistress of the house.' At this time, therefore, perhaps ten o'clock on Sunday morning, you see that Spinosa was alive, and pretty well. But it seems 'he had summoned from Amsterdam a certain physician, whom,' says the biographer, 'I shall not otherwise point out to notice than by these two letters, L. M. This L. M. had directed the people of the house to purchase an ancient cock, and to have him boiled forthwith, in order that Spinosa might take some broth about noon, which in fact he did, and ate some of the *old cock* with a good appetite, after the landlord and his wife had returned from church.'

'In the afternoon, L. M. staid alone with Spinosa, the people of the house having returned to church; on coming out from which they learnt, with much surprise, that Spinosa had died about three o'clock, in the presence of L. M., who took his departure for Amsterdam the same evening, by the night-boat, without paying the least attention to the deceased. No doubt he was the readier to dispense with these duties, as he had possessed himself of a ducatoon and a small quantity of silver, together with a silver-hafted knife, and had absconded with his pillage.' Here you see, gentlemen, the murder is plain, and the manner of it. It was L. M. who murdered Spinosa for his money. Poor S. was an invalid, meagre, and weak: as no blood was observed, L. M., no doubt, threw him down and smothered him with pillows, – the poor man being already half suffocated by his infernal dinner. – But who was L. M.? It surely never could be Lindley Murray; for I saw him at York in 1825; and besides, I do not think he would do such a thing; at least, not to a brother grammarian: for you know, gentlemen, that Spinosa wrote a very respectable Hebrew grammar.

Hobbes, but why, or on what principle, I never could understand, was not murdered. This was a capital oversight of the professional men in the seventeenth century; because in every light he was a fine subject for murder, except, indeed, that he was lean and skinny; for I can prove that he had money, and (what is very funny,) he had no right to make the least resistance; for, according to himself, irresistible power creates the very highest species of right, so that it is rebellion of the blackest die to refuse to be murdered, when a competent force appears to murder you. However, gentlemen, though he was not murdered, I am happy to assure you that (by his own account,) he was three times very near being murdered. – The first time was in the spring of 1640, when he pretends to have circulated a little MS. on the king's behalf, against the Parliament; he never could produce this MS., by the by; but he says that, 'had not his Majesty dissolved the Parliament,' (in May,) 'it had brought him into danger of his life.' Dissolving the Parliament, however, was of no use; for, in November of the same year, the Long Parliament assembled, and Hobbes, a second time, fearing he should be murdered, ran away to France. This looks like the madness of John Dennis, who thought that Louis XIV. would never make peace with Queen Anne, unless he were given up to his vengeance; and actually ran away from the sea-coast in that belief. In France, Hobbes managed to take care of his throat pretty well for ten years; but at the end of that time, by way of paying court to Cromwell, he published his Leviathan. The old coward now began to 'funk' horribly for the third time; he fancied the swords of the cavaliers were constantly at his throat, recollecting how they had served the Parliament ambassadors at the Hague and Madrid. 'Tum,' says he, in his dog-Latin life of himself,

> Tum venit in mentem mihi Dorislaus et Ascham;
> Tanquam proscripto terror ubique aderat.
> ['Then I began thinking about Dorislaus and Ascham
> Terror was all around, as for someone condemned
> to death']

And accordingly he ran home to England. Now, certainly, it is very true that a man deserved a cudgelling for writing Leviathan; and two or three cudgellings for writing a pentameter ending so villainously as – 'terror ubique aderat!' But no man ever thought him worthy of any thing beyond cudgelling. And, in fact, the whole story is a bounce of his own. For, in a most abusive letter which he wrote 'to a learned person,' (meaning Wallis the mathematician,) he gives quite another account of the matter, and says

(p. 8.), he ran home 'because he would not trust his safety with the French clergy;' insinuating that he was likely to be murdered for his religion, which would have been a high joke indeed – Tom's being brought to the stake for religion.

Bounce or not bounce, however, certain it is, that Hobbes, to the end of his life, feared that somebody would murder him. This is proved by the story I am going to tell you: it is not from a manuscript, but, (as Mr Coleridge says), it is as good as manuscript; for it comes from a book now entirely forgotten, viz. – 'The Creed of Mr Hobbes Examined; in a Conference between him and a Student in Divinity,' (published about ten years before Hobbes's death.) The book is anonymous, but it was written by Tennison, the same who, about thirty years after, succeeded Tillotson as Archbishop of Canterbury. The introductory anecdote is as follows: – 'A certain divine, it seems, (no doubt Tennison himself,) took an annual tour of one month to different parts of the island. In one of these excursions (1670) he visited the Peak in Derbyshire, partly in consequence of Hobbes's description of it. Being in that neighbourhood, he could not but pay a visit to Buxton; and at the very moment of his arrival, he was fortunate enough to find a party of gentlemen dismounting at the inn door, amongst whom was a long thin fellow, who turned out to be no less a person than Mr Hobbes, who probably had ridden over from Chattsworth. Meeting so great a lion, – a tourist, in search of the picturesque, could do no less than present himself in the character of bore. And luckily for this scheme, two of Mr Hobbes's companions were suddenly summoned away by express; so that, for the rest of his stay at Buxton, he had Leviathan entirely to himself, and had the honour of bowsing with him in the evening. Hobbes, it seems, at first showed a good deal of stiffness, for he was shy of divines; but this wore off, and he became very sociable and funny, and they agreed to go into the bath together.' How Tennison could venture to gambol in the same water with Leviathan, I cannot explain; but so it was: they frolicked about like two dolphins, though Hobbes must have been as old as the hills; and 'in those intervals wherein they abstained from swimming and plunging themselves,' (i.e. diving) 'they discoursed of many things relating to the Baths of the Ancients, and the Origine of Springs. When they had in this manner passed away an hour, they stepped out of the bath; and, having dried and cloathed themselves, they sate down in expectation of such a supper as the place afforded; designing to refresh themselves like the *Deipnosophilae*, and rather to reason than to drink profoundly. But in this innocent intention they were interrupted by the disturbance arising from a little quarrel, in which some of the ruder people in the house were for a short time engaged. At this Mr Hobbes seemed much concerned, though he was at some distance from the persons.' – And why was he concerned, gentlemen? No doubt you fancy, from some benign and disinterested love of peace and harmony, worthy of an old man and a philosopher. But listen – 'For a while he was not composed, but related it once or twice as to himself, with a low and careful tone, how Sextus Roscius was murthered after supper by the Balneae Palatinae. Of such general extent is that remark of Cicero, in relation to Epicurus the Atheist, of whom he observed that he of all men dreaded most those things which he contemned – Death and the Gods.' – Merely because it was supper-time, and in the neighbourhood of a bath, Mr Hobbes must have the fate of Sextus Roscius. What logic was there in this, unless to a man who was always dreaming of murder? – Here was Leviathan, no longer afraid of the daggers of English cavaliers or French clergy, but 'frightened from his propriety' by a row in an ale-house between some honest clod-hoppers of Derbyshire, whom his own gaunt scare-crow of a person that belonged to quite another century, would have frightened out of their wits.

Malebranche, it will give you pleasure to hear, was murdered. The man who murdered him is well known: it was Bishop Berkeley. The story is familiar, though hitherto not put in a proper light. Berkeley, when a young man, went to Paris and called on Père Malebranche. He found him in his cell cooking. Cooks have ever been a *genus irritabile*; authors still more so: Malebranche was both: a dispute arose; the old Father, warm already, became warmer; culinary and metaphysical irritations united to derange his liver: he took to his bed, and died. Such is the common version of the story: 'So the whole ear of Denmark is abused.' – The fact is, that the matter was hushed up, out of consideration for Berkeley, who (as Pope remarked) had 'every virtue under heaven:' else it was well known that Berkeley, feeling himself nettled by the waspishness of the old Frenchman, squared at him; a *turn-up* was the consequence: Malebranche was floored in the first round; the conceit was wholly taken out of him; and he would perhaps have given in; but Berkeley's blood was now up, and he insisted on the old Frenchman's retracting his doctrine of Occasional Causes. The vanity of the man was too great for this; and he fell a sacrifice to the impetuosity of Irish youth, combined with his own absurd obstinacy.

Leibnitz, being every way superior to Malebranche, one might, *a fortiori*, have counted on *his* being murdered; which, however, was not the case. I believe he was nettled at this neglect, and felt himself insulted by the security in which he passed his days. In no other way can I explain his conduct at the latter end of his life, when he chose to grow very avaricious, and to hoard up large sums of gold, which he kept in his own house. This was at Vienna, where he died; and letters are still in existence, describing the immeasurable anxiety which he entertained for his throat. Still his ambition, for being *attempted* at least, was so great, that he would not forego the danger. A late English pedagogue, of Birmingham manufacture, viz. Dr Parr, took a more selfish course, under the same circumstances. He had amassed a considerable quantity of gold and silver plate, which was for some time deposited in his bed-room at his parsonage house, Hatton. But growing every day more afraid of being murdered, which he knew that he could not stand, (and to which, indeed, he never had the slightest pretension,) he transferred the whole to the Hatton blacksmith; conceiving, no doubt, that the murder of a blacksmith would fall more lightly on the *salus reipublicae* [the safety of the republic], than that of a pedagogue. But I have heard this greatly disputed; and it seems now generally agreed, that one good horse-shoe is worth about 2¼ Spital sermons.

As Leibnitz, though not murdered, may be said to have died, partly of the fear that he should be murdered, and partly of vexation that he was not, – Kant, on the other hand – who had no ambition in that way – had a narrower escape from a murderer than any man we read of, except Des Cartes. So absurdly does Fortune throw about her favours! The case is told, I think, in an anonymous life of this very great man. For health's sake, Kant imposed upon himself, at one time, a walk of six miles every day along a highroad. This fact becoming known to a man who had his private reasons for committing murder, at the third milestone from Königsberg, he waited for his 'intended,' who came up to time as duly as a mail-coach. But for an accident, Kant was a dead man. However, on considerations of 'morality,' it happened that the murderer preferred a little child, whom he saw playing in the road, to the old transcendentalist: this child he murdered; and thus it happened that Kant escaped. Such is the German account of the matter; but my opinion is – that the murderer was an amateur, who felt how little would be gained to the cause of good taste by murdering an old, arid, and adust metaphysician; there was no room for display, as the man could not possibly look more like a mummy when dead, than he had done alive.

Thus, gentlemen, I have traced the connexion between philosophy and our art, until insensibly I find that I have wandered into our own era. This I shall not take any pains to characterise apart from that which preceded it, for, in fact, they have no distinct character. The 17th and 18th centuries, together with so much of the 19th as we have yet seen, jointly compose the Augustan age of murder. The finest work of the 17th century is, unquestionably, the murder of Sir Edmondbury Godfrey, which has my entire approbation. At the same time, it must be observed, that the quantity of murder was not great in this century, at least amongst our own artists; which, perhaps, is attributable to the want of enlightened patronage. *Sint Maecenates, non deerunt, Flacce, Marones* ['Let there be a patron like Maecenus, Flaccus, and your lands will give you a poet like Virgil.'] Consulting Grant's 'Observations on the Bills of Mortality,' (4th edition, Oxford, 1665,) I find, that out of 229,250, who died in London during one period of twenty years in the 17th century, not more than eighty-six were murdered; that is, about 4 three-tenths per annum. A small number this, gentlemen, to found an academy upon; and certainly, where the quantity is so small, we have a right to expect that the quality should be first-rate. Perhaps it was; yet, still I am of opinion that the best artist in this century was not equal to the best in that which followed. For instance, however praiseworthy the case of Sir Edmondbury Godfrey may be (and nobody can be more sensible of its merits than I am,) still I cannot consent to place it on a level with that Mrs Ruscombe of Bristol, either as to originality of design, or boldness and breadth of style. This good lady's murder took place early in the reign of George III. – a reign which was notoriously favourable to the arts generally. She lived in College Green, with a single maid-servant, neither of them having any pretension to the notice of history but what they derived from the great artist whose workmanship I am recording. One fine morning, when all Bristol was alive and in motion, some suspicion arising, the neighbours forced an entrance into the house, and found Mrs Ruscombe murdered in her bed-room, and the servant murdered on the stairs: this was at noon; and, not more than two hours before, both mistress and servant had been seen alive. To the best of my remembrance, this was in 1764; upwards of sixty years, therefore, have now elapsed, and yet the artist is still undiscovered. The suspicions of posterity have settled upon two pretenders – a baker and a chimney-sweeper. But posterity is wrong; no unpractised artist could have conceived so bold an idea as that of a noon-day murder in the heart of a great city. It was no obscure baker, gentlemen, or anonymous chimney-sweeper, be assured, that executed this work. I know who it was. (*Here there was a general buzz, which at length broke out into open applause; upon which the lecturer blushed, and went on with much earnestness.*) For Heaven's sake, gentlemen, do not mistake me; it was not I that did it. I have not the vanity to think myself equal to any such achievement; be assured that you greatly overrate my poor talents; Mrs Ruscombe's affair was far beyond my slender abilities. But I came to know who the artist was, from a celebrated surgeon, who assisted at his dissection. This gentleman had a private museum in the way of his profession, one corner of which was occupied by a cast from a man of remarkably fine proportions.

'That,' said the surgeon, 'is a cast from the celebrated Lancashire highwayman, who concealed his profession for some time from his neighbours, by drawing woollen stockings over his horse's legs, and in that way muffling the clatter which he must else have made in riding up a flagged alley that led to his stable. At the time of his execution for highway robbery, I was studying under Cruickshank: and the man's figure was so uncommonly fine, that no money or exertion was spared to get into possession of him with the least possible delay. By the connivance of the under-sheriff he was cut down within the legal time, and instantly put into a chaise and four; so that, when he reached Cruickshank's, he was positively not dead. Mr —, a young student at that time, had the honour of giving him the *coup de grace* – and finishing the sentence of the law.' This remarkable anecdote, which seemed to imply that all the gentlemen in the dissecting-room were amateurs of our class, struck me a good deal; and I was repeating it one day to a Lancashire lady, who thereupon informed me, that she had herself lived in the neighbourhood of that highwayman, and well remembered two circumstances, which combined in the opinion of all his neighbours, to fix upon him the credit of Mrs Ruscombe's affair. One was, the fact of his absence for a whole fortnight at the period of that murder: the other, that, within a very little time after, the neighbourhood of this highwayman was deluged with dollars: now Mrs Ruscombe was known to have hoarded about two thousand of that coin. Be the artist, however, who he might, the affair remains a durable monument of his genius; for such was the impression of awe, and the sense of power left behind, by the strength of conception manifested in this murder, that no tenant (as I was told in 1810) had been found up to that time for Mrs Ruscombe's house.

But, whilst I thus eulogize the Ruscombian case, let me not be supposed to overlook the many other specimens of extraordinary merit spread over the face of this century. Such cases, indeed, as that of Miss Bland, or of Captain Donnellan, and Sir Theophilus Boughton, shall never have any countenance from me. Fie on these dealers in poison, say I: can they not keep to the old honest way of cutting throats, without introducing such abominable innovations from Italy? I consider all these poisoning cases, compared with the legitimate style, as no better than wax-work by the side of sculpture, or a lithographic print by the side of a fine Volpato. But, dismissing these, there remain many excellent works of art in a pure style, such as nobody need be ashamed to own, as every candid connoisseur will admit. *Candid*, observe, I say; for great allowances must be made in these cases; no artist can ever be sure of carrying through his own fine preconception. Awkward disturbances will arise; people will not submit to have their throats cut quietly; they will run, they will kick, they will bite;

and, whilst the portrait painter often has to complain of too much torpor in his subject, the artist, in our line, is generally embarrassed by too much animation. At the same time, however disagreeable to the artist, this tendency in murder to excite and irritate the subject, is certainly one of its advantages to the world in general, which we ought not to overlook, since it favours the developement of latent talent. Jeremy Taylor notices with admiration, the extraordinary leaps which people will take under the influence of fear. There was a striking instance of this in the recent case of the M'Keands; the boy cleared a height, such as he will never clear again to his dying day. Talents also of the most brilliant description for thumping, and indeed for all the gymnastic exercises, have sometimes been developed by the panic which accompanies our artists; talents else buried and hid under a bushel to the possessors, as much as to their friends. I remember an interesting illustration of this fact, in a case which I learned in Germany.

Riding one day in the neighbourhood of Munich, I overtook a distinguished amateur of our society, whose name I shall conceal. This gentleman informed me that, finding himself wearied with the frigid pleasures (so he called them) of mere amateurship, he had quitted England for the continent – meaning to practise a little professionally. For this purpose he resorted to Germany, conceiving the police in that part of Europe to be more heavy and drowsy than elsewhere. His *debut* as a practitioner took place at Mannheim; and, knowing me to be a brother amateur, he freely communicated the whole of his maiden adventure. 'Opposite to my lodging,' said he, 'lived a baker: he was somewhat of a miser, and lived quite alone. Whether it were his great expanse of chalky face, or what else, I know not – but the fact was, I "fancied" him, and resolved to commence business upon his throat, which by the way he always carried bare – a fashion which is very irritating to my desires. Precisely at eight o'clock in the evening, I observed that he regularly shut up his windows. One night I watched him when thus engaged – bolted in after him – locked the door – and, addressing him with great suavity, acquainted him with the nature of my errand; at the same time advising him to make no resistance, which would be mutually unpleasant. So saying, I drew out my tools; and was proceeding to operate. But at this spectacle, the baker, who seemed to have been struck by catalepsy at my first announce, awoke into tremendous agitation. "I will *not* be murdered!" he shrieked aloud; "what for will I lose my precious throat?" – "What for?" said I; "if for no other reason, for this – that you put alum into your bread. But no matter, alum or no alum, (for I was resolved to forestall any argument on that point) know that I am a virtuoso in the art of murder – am desirous of improving myself in its details – and am enamoured of your vast surface of throat, to which I am determined to be a customer." "Is it so?" said he, "but I'll find you custom in another line;" and so saying, he threw himself into a boxing attitude. The very idea of his boxing struck me as ludicrous. It is true, a London baker had distinguished himself in the ring, and became known to fame under the title of the Master of the Rolls; but he was young and unspoiled: whereas this man was a monstrous feather-bed in person, fifty years old, and totally out of condition. Spite of all this, however, and contending against me, who am a master in the art, he made so desperate a defence, that many times I feared he might turn the tables upon me; and that I, an amateur, might be murdered by a rascally baker. What a situation!

Minds of sensibility will sympathize with my anxiety. How severe it was, you may understand by this, that for the first 13 rounds the baker had the advantage. Round the 14th, I received a blow on the right eye, which closed it up; in the end, I believe, this was my salvation: for the anger it roused in me was so great that, in this and every one of the three following rounds, I floored the baker.

'Round 18th. The baker came up piping, and manifestly the worse for wear. His geometrical exploits in the four last rounds had done him no good. However, he showed some skill in stopping a message which I was sending to his cadaverous mug; in delivering which, my foot slipped, and I went down.

'Round 19th. Surveying the baker, I became ashamed of having been so much bothered by a shapeless mass of dough; and I went in fiercely, and administered some severe punishment. A rally took place – both went down – Baker undermost – ten to three on Amateur.

'Round 20th. – The baker jumped up with surprising agility; indeed, he managed his pins capitally, and fought wonderfully, considering that he was drenched in perspiration; but the shine was now taken out of him, and his game was the mere effect of panic. It was now clear that he could not last much longer. In the course of this round we tried the weaving system, in which I had greatly the advantage, and hit him repeatedly on the conk. My reason for this was, that his conk was covered with carbuncles; and I thought I should vex him by taking such liberties with his conk, which in fact I did.

'The three next rounds, the master of the rolls staggered about like a cow on the ice. Seeing how matters stood, in round 24th I whispered something into his ear, which sent him down like a shot. It was nothing more than my private opinion of the value of his throat at an annuity office. This little confidential whisper affected him greatly; the very perspiration was frozen on his face, and for the next two rounds I had it all my own way. And when I called *time* for the twenty-seventh round, he lay like a log on the floor.'

After which, said I to the amateur, 'It may be presumed that you accomplished your purpose.' – 'You are right,' said he mildly, 'I did; and a great satisfaction, you know, it was to my mind, for by this means I killed two birds with one stone;' meaning that he had both thumped the baker and murdered him. Now, for the life of me, I could not see *that*; for, on the contrary, to my mind it appeared that he had taken two stones to kill one bird, having been obliged to take the conceit out of him first with his fists, and then with his tools. But no matter for his logic. The moral of his story was good, for it showed what an astonishing stimulus to latent talent is contained in any reasonable prospect of being murdered. A pursy, unwieldy, half cataleptic baker of Mannheim had absolutely fought six-and-twenty rounds with an accomplished English boxer merely upon this inspiration; so greatly was natural genius exalted and sublimed by the genial presence of his murderer.

Really, gentlemen, when one hears of such things as these, it becomes a duty, perhaps, a little to soften that extreme asperity with which most men speak of murder. To hear people talk, you would suppose that all the disadvantages and inconveniences were on the side of being murdered, and that there were none at all in *not* being murdered. But considerate men think otherwise. 'Certainly,' says Jer. Taylor, 'it is a less temporal evil to fall by the rudeness of a sword than the violence of a fever: and the axe' (to which he might have added the ship-carpenter's mallet and the crow-bar) 'a much less affliction than a strangury.' Very true; the Bishop talks like a wise man and an amateur, as he is; and another great philosopher, Marcus Aurelius, was equally above the vulgar prejudices on this subject. He declares it to be one of 'the noblest functions of reason to know whether it is time to walk out of the world or not.' (Book III. Collers' Translation.) No sort of knowledge being rarer than this, surely *that* man must be a most philanthropic character, who undertakes to instruct people in this branch of knowledge gratis, and at no little hazard to himself. All this, however, I throw out only in the way of speculation to future moralists; declaring in the meantime my own private conviction, that very few men commit murder upon philanthropic or patriotic principles, and repeating what I have already said once at least – that, as to the majority of murderers, they are very incorrect characters.

With respect to Williams's murders, the sublimest and most entire in their excellence that ever were committed, I shall not allow myself to speak incidentally. Nothing less than an entire lecture, or even an entire course of lectures, would suffice to expound their merits. But one curious fact, connected with his case, I shall mention, because it seems to imply that the blaze of his genius absolutely dazzled the eye of criminal justice. You all remember, I doubt not, that the instruments with which he executed his first great work (the murder of the Marrs), were a ship-carpenter's mallet and a knife. Now the mallet belonged to an old Swede, one John Petersen, and bore his initials. This instrument Williams left behind him, in Marr's house, and it fell into the hands of the Magistrates. Now, gentlemen, it is a fact that the publication of this circumstance of the initials led immediately to the apprehension of Williams, and, if made earlier, would have prevented his second great work, (the murder of the Williamsons,) which took place precisely twelve days after. But the Magistrates kept back this fact from the public for the entire twelve days, and until that second work was accomplished. That finished, they published it, apparently feeling that Williams had now done enough for his fame, and that his glory was at length placed beyond the reach of accident.

As to Mr Thurtell's case, I know not what to say. Naturally, I have every disposition to think highly of my predecessor in the chair of this society; and I acknowledge that his lectures were unexceptionable. But, speaking ingenuously, I do really think that his principal performance, as an artist, has been much overrated. I admit that at first I was myself carried away by the general enthusiasm. On the morning when the murder was made known in London, there was the fullest meeting of amateurs that I have ever known since the days of Williams; old bed-ridden connoisseurs, who had got into a peevish way of sneering and complaining 'that there was nothing doing,' now hobbled down to our club-room: such hilarity, such benign expression of general satisfaction, I have rarely witnessed. On every side you saw people shaking hands, congratulating each other, and forming dinner-parties for the evening; and nothing was to be heard but triumphant challenges of – 'Well! will *this* do?' 'Is *this* the right thing?' 'Are you satisfied at last?' But, in the midst of this, I remember we all grew silent on hearing the old cynical amateur, L. S——, that *laudator temporis acti* [a praiser of time past], stumping along with his wooden leg; he entered the room with his usual scowl, and, as he advanced, he continued to growl and stutter the whole way – 'Not an original idea in the whole piece – mere plagiarism, – base plagiarism from hints that I threw out! Besides, his style is as hard as Albert Durer, and as coarse as Fuseli.' Many thought that this was mere jealousy, and general waspishness; but I confess that, when the first glow of enthusiasm had subsided, I have found most judicious critics to agree that there was something *falsetto* in the style of Thurtell. The fact is, he was a member of our society, which naturally gave a friendly bias to our judgments; and his person was universally familiar to the cockneys, which gave him, with the whole London public, a temporary popularity, that his pretensions are not capable of supporting; for *opinionum commenta delet dies, naturae judicia confirmat* ['Time erases the fictions of opinion, but it confirms the judgements of nature']. – There was, however, an unfinished design of Thurtell's for the murder of a man with a pair of dumb-bells, which I admired greatly; it was a mere outline, that he never completed; but to my mind it seemed every way superior to his chief work. I remember that there was great regret expressed by some amateurs that this sketch should have been left in an unfinished state: but there I cannot agree with them; for the

49

fragments and first bold outlines of original artists have often a felicity about them which is apt to vanish in the management of the details.

The case of the M'Keands I consider far beyond the vaunted performance of Thurtell, – indeed above all praise; and bearing that relation, in fact, to the immortal works of Williams, which the Aeneid bears to the Iliad.

But it is now time that I should say a few words about the principles of murder, not with a view to regulate your practice, but your judgment: as to old women, and the mob of newspaper readers, they are pleased with anything, provided it is bloody enough. But the mind of sensibility requires something more. *First*, then, let us speak of the kind of person who is adapted to the purpose of the murderer; *secondly*, of the place where; *thirdly*, of the time when, and other little circumstances.

As to the person, I suppose it is evident that he ought to be a good man; because, if he were not, he might himself, by possibility, be contemplating murder at the very time; and such 'diamond-cut-diamond' tussles, though pleasant enough where nothing better is stirring, are really not what a critic can allow himself to call murders. I could mention some people (I name no names) who have been murdered by other people in a dark lane; and so far all seemed correct enough; but, on looking farther into the matter, the public have become aware that the murdered party was himself, at the moment, planning to rob his murderer, at the least, and possibly to murder him, if he had been strong enough. Whenever that is the case, or may be thought to be the case, farewell to all the genuine effects of the art. For the final purpose of murder, considered as a fine art, is precisely the same as that of Tragedy, in Aristotle's account of it, viz. 'to cleanse the heart by means of pity and terror.' Now, terror there may be, but how can there be any pity for one tiger destroyed by another tiger?

It is also evident that the person selected ought not to be a public character. For instance, no judicious artist would have attempted to murder Abraham Newland. For the case was this: everybody read so much about Abraham Newland, and so few people ever saw him, that there was a fixed belief that he was an abstract idea. And I remember that once, when

I happened to mention that I had dined at a coffee-house in company with Abraham Newland, everybody looked scornfully at me, as though I had pretended to have played at billiards with Prester John, or to have had an affair of honour with the Pope. And, by the way, the Pope would be a very improper person to murder: for he has such a virtual ubiquity as the Father of Christendom, and, like the cuckoo, is so often heard but never seen, that I suspect most people regard *him* also as an abstract idea. Where, indeed, a public character is in the habit of giving dinners, 'with every delicacy of the season,' the case is very different: every person is satisfied that *he* is no abstract idea; and, therefore, there can be no impropriety in murdering him; only that his murder will fall into the class of assassinations, which I have not yet treated.

Thirdly, The subject chosen ought to be in good health: for it is absolutely barbarous to murder a sick person, who is usually quite unable to bear it. On this principle, no Cockney ought to be chosen who is above twenty-five, for after that age he is sure to be dyspeptic. Or at least, if a man will hunt in that warren, he ought to murder a couple at one time; if the Cockneys chosen should be tailors, he will of course think it his duty, on the old established equation, to murder eighteen – And, here, in this attention to the comfort of sick people, you will observe the usual effect of a fine art to soften and refine the feelings. The world in general, gentlemen, are very bloody-minded; and all they want in a murder is a copious effusion of blood; gaudy display in this point is enough for *them*. But the enlightened connoisseur is more refined in his taste; and from our art, as from all the other liberal arts when thoroughly cultivated, the result is – to improve and to humanize the heart; so true is it, that –

> – Ingenuas didicisse fideliter artes,
> Emollit mores, nec sinit esse feros.
> ['A careful study of the liberal arts refines
> manners and prevents them from being savage']

A philosophic friend, well-known for his philanthropy and general benignity, suggests that the subject chosen ought also to have a family of young children wholly dependent on his exertions, by way of deepening the pathos. And, undoubtedly, this is a judicious caution. Yet I would not insist too keenly on this condition. Severe good taste unquestionably demands it; but still, where the man was otherwise unobjectionable in point of morals and health, I would not look with too curious a jealousy to a restriction which might have the effect of narrowing the artist's sphere.

So much for the person. As to the time, the place, and the tools, I have many things to say, which at present I have no room for. The good sense of the practitioner has usually directed him to night and privacy. Yet there have not been wanting cases where this rule was departed from with excellent effect. In respect to time, Mrs Ruscombe's case is a beautiful exception, which I have already noticed; and in respect both to time and place, there is a fine exception in the Annals of Edinburgh, (year 1805), familiar to every child in Edinburgh, but which has unaccountably been defrauded of its due portion of fame amongst English amateurs. The case I mean is that of a porter to one of the Banks, who was murdered whilst carrying a bag of money, in broad daylight, on turning out of the High Street, one of the most public streets in Europe, and the murderer is to this hour undiscovered.

Sed fugit interea, fugit irreparabile tempus,
Singula dum capti circumvectamur amore.
['But meanwhile time is flying, flying beyond recall,
while we linger, captivated by our love of detail']

And now, gentlemen, in conclusion, let me again
solemnly disclaim all pretensions on my own part to
the character of a professional man. I never attempted
any murder in my life, except in the year 1801, upon
the body of a tom-cat; and *that* turned out differently
from my intention. My purpose, I own, was downright murder. 'Semper ego auditor tantum?' said I,
'nunquamne reponam?' ['Am I always to be a listener?
And never get a word in?'] And I went down stairs in
search of Tom at one o'clock on a dark night, with
the 'animus,' and no doubt with the fiendish looks,
of a murderer. But when I found him, he was in the
act of plundering the pantry of bread and other
things. Now this gave a new turn to the affair; for the
time being one of general scarcity, when even Chris-
tians were reduced to the use of potato-bread,
rice-bread, and all sorts of things, it was downright
treason in a tom-cat to be wasting good wheaten-bread
in the way he was doing. It instantly became a

patriotic duty to put him to death; and as I raised aloft and shook the glittering steel, I fancied myself rising like Brutus, effulgent from a crowd of patriots, and, as I stabbed him, I

> called aloud on Tully's name,
> And bade the father of his country hail!

Since then, what wandering thoughts I may have had of attempting the life of an ancient ewe, of a superannuated hen, and such 'small deer,' are locked up in the secrets of my own breast; but for the higher departments of the art, I confess myself to be utterly unfit. My ambition does not rise so high. No, gentlemen, in the words of Horace,

> ———fungar vice cotis, acutum
Reddere quae ferrum valet, exsors ipsa secandi.
['I'll play the part of a whetstone, which sharpens iron, but is itself unable to cut.']